This book belongs to

....

....

....

....

This is a Bright Sparks Book.
First published 2000
Bright Sparks
Queen Street House,
4, Queen Street,
Bath, BA1 1HE, UK.
Copyright © Parragon 2000

Produced for Parragon Books by
Oyster Books Ltd, Unit 4, Kirklea Farm,
Badgworth, Somerset, BS26 2QH, UK

Illustrated by Andrew Geeson
Written by Marilyn Tolhurst

Printed in Italy

ISBN 1 84250 061 9

A FRIEND FOR BARNEY

Illustrated by Andrew Geeson

Bright ☆ Sparks

It was Saturday morning at Faraway Farm.
Danny, Rosie and Conker the dog went down to the
pond to feed some breadcrumbs to the ducks.

"All the ducks are friends," said Rosie. "They never fight about who gets the biggest piece."

"Not like you," said Danny.

"That's because you always get the biggest piece," said Rosie.

When they went to see the chickens, Danny asked, "Are they friends too?"

"I think so," said Rosie, "but some of them are a bit pecky."

"What about the pigs? Sometimes Bessie can be a bit grumpy with her piglets," said Danny.

"Oh, that's just because she is their mum," said Rosie, "and they are very greedy sometimes so Bessie has to tell them off. She is very friendly really."

"Everybody at Faraway Farm has friends," agreed Danny. "Even the red tractor is friends with the old blue van."

"My best friend is Stan," said Rosie.

"Cats are boring," declared Danny. "They just sleep all the time. My best friend is Conker. He is the fastest dog in the world and he can catch sticks in the air. Watch this!"

"But Barney the scarecrow doesn't have a friend," said Rosie frowning. "He just stands on the hill all day with no one to talk to."

"Let's go and see him."

When they went back to the house, Rosie said to her Mum,
"Barney's lonely. I want him to have a friend."

"Then why don't you make him one?" asked Mum.

In the afternoon, Mum took them to a jumble sale in town
so they could get some clothes for a new scarecrow.

JUMBLE SALE

Danny found an old pair of sports shoes and a pair of motorbike gloves.

Rosie found a nice pink party dress and a hat with a green ribbon.

They asked Dad if he would help them to make a scarecrow. "Yes," said Dad. "All we need is a sack and some straw and a big pumpkin."

Danny stuffed the sack with straw and Dad helped Rosie to paint a face on the pumpkin. "She looks friendly already," smiled Rosie.

"But she'll still scare the birds," said Danny.

Mum made some hair out of wool, then she found a
necklace and a bright blue handbag.
"What a beauty," said Dad. "All she needs is a name."

"I want to call her Mary, like my favourite dolly," said Rosie.

"Scary Mary Crow," said Danny. "That's a great name."
So, that's what they called her.

They took Scary Mary up the hill.
"Hello Barney," greeted Danny.
"We've brought you a friend."
"Now you won't be lonely any more,"
added Rosie.

"I think Barney likes her," said Danny.

"He can see by looking at the boots she is wearing that she's very good at football."

"I think he likes her because she has a smiley face," said Rosie.

Dad put some money in Barney's pocket and some more in Mary's handbag.

"Now they can go to the beach and buy an ice cream," he said.

Rosie skipped all the way home to tell Stan the cat all about Scary Mary.

"I'm very happy, Stan," she said giving him a big hug. "Now everybody at Faraway Farm has got a friend."